OZZIE OWL ON THE MOON

BY JUNE WOODMAN
ILLUSTRATED BY PAMELA STOREY

Brimax Books · Newmarket · England

Ozzie Owl is very clever.
He can fly high and low.
He can fly fast and slow.
"You are very clever,"
say the little ducklings.
"I wish I could fly,"
says Cuddly Cat.
"We wish we could fly," say
Bossy Bear and Paddy Dog.
"We cannot fly," say Hoppy
Rabbit, Flippy Frog and
Merry Mole.

"Yes," says Ozzie, "I am very good at flying.
I can fly high and low.
I can fly fast and slow.
But I cannot fly to the moon."
"You are silly," says Dilly Duck. "Owls do not go to the moon."
"But I want to go," says Ozzie. "I want to be the first owl on the moon."

"Owls CANNOT go to the moon," says Dilly Duck. "They cannot go to sleep with all this chatter," says Ozzie Owl. He flies up into his tree. He is very cross. "Come with me," says Hoppy. "I know a secret place, and I will show you." So they all get into Hoppy's car, and away they go.

It is a long way to Hoppy's
place, but at last they get
to it. It is very rocky.
There are no flowers. There
are no trees, and there is
no grass. It is very bare.
"This is my secret place,"
says Hoppy, "Do you like it?"
"We like it," say the three
little ducklings.
"It is just like the moon!" say
Paddy, Merry and Flippy.

"I play space games here,"
says Hoppy. "Look at my
space helmet. See how
I make my car look like
a space buggy."
Hoppy puts on his helmet.
He puts silver paper all
round his car. It looks
good.
"It looks just like a space
buggy," say Flippy Frog
and Merry Mole.

"Come back to my house," says Cuddly. "I have a big box full of old things. We can all make space suits." Bossy has some tins of paint. There is silver paint, too. So they take all the paint to Cuddly's house. Then they get all the old things from Cuddly's big box, and set to work.

Cuddly has lots of old boots.
She paints them silver.
"They make good space boots," she says.
Bossy and Hoppy get a very big box, and make a space rocket. Flippy, Merry and Paddy Dog make space suits for everyone. Dilly makes ray guns. The three little ducklings help, but they get paint all over them.

"It all looks good," they say.
They put the rocket into the
space buggy. Then they put
on the space suits, and pick
up the ray guns.
"Time to go and get Ozzie,"
says Hoppy.
They all get into the space
buggy, and away they go.
"This is good fun," say the
three little ducklings.

They go to the forest, but
Ozzie is asleep in the tree.
"What can we do now?"
says Cuddly Cat.
"Help me," says Hoppy.
"Then we can lift him down."
Bossy and Paddy run to help.
They lift Ozzie down from
the tree. He is still asleep.
They put him in the back
of the space buggy.
He is STILL asleep.

They all get into the buggy, and Hoppy takes them back to his secret place. They run and play with all the space things.

The buggy is at the top of a little hill. Dilly Duck looks at it. It begins to go. It goes fast down the hill.

"Help!" says Dilly. "The buggy is running away!"

BUMP!
Ozzie wakes up, and looks
all round. He sees a rocky
place, with no grass and no
trees. He can see a space
rocket. He can see space men
with ray guns, too.
They run up to him.
"Help!" hoots Ozzie Owl.
"Am I on the moon?
I do not like it here!"

The buggy hits a big rock. BUMP!
Ozzie Owl falls out of the silver buggy. He lands with a big bump.
"OOOOOOH!" hoots Ozzie, "I do not like the moon. I want to go home."
Dilly runs to help him.
"The space men will get me!" says Ozzie.
"You ARE silly," says Dilly.

They all run up to Ozzie,
and take off their space
helmets.
"We are playing space men,"
say Bossy, Paddy and Hoppy.
"I will not go to the moon,"
says Ozzie, "but I will play
space games with you."
So they all stay and play.
They have lots of fun till
Dilly Duck says, "Home time!"

Say these words again

clever

flying

chatter

secret

place

rocky

grass

suits

space

silver

paper

round

could

asleep